WAYANS FAMILY PRESENTS

Amy HODGEPODGE
DIGGING UP TROUBLE

BY KIM WAYANS & KEVIN KNOTTS
ILLUSTRATED BY SOO JEONG

SCHOLASTIC INC.
New York Toronto London Auckland
Sydney Mexico City New Delhi Hong Kong

For Elvira, Howell, Billie, and Ivan.
And for Sylvia—the best teacher ever.

ISBN 978-0-545-35142-3

12 11 10 9 8 7 6 5 4 3 2   11 12 13 14 15 16/0

Printed in the U.S.A.   40

First Scholastic printing, March 2011

Chapter 1

"That was the coolest assembly ever!" I exclaimed as I sat down at my usual table in the cafeteria. Some of my friends were already there—Lola, Pia, Maya, Jesse, and Rusty. The only one missing was Lola's twin brother, Cole. He was still in the lunch line.

That morning, the entire fourth grade had heard a lecture by a special guest speaker. Her name was Ms. Thorner, and she'd talked all about the importance of being "green" and taking care of the environment.

"I know, right?" Lola agreed as she unwrapped her turkey sandwich. "My new favorite color is green."

"Green is totally in," Pia said. She looked down at her clothes. She was wearing a cute blue dress. Pia is probably the most stylish person in the entire school. "Hmm. Maybe I should go shopping for some new green accessories."

Lola grinned. "You always want to go shopping!"

Lola loved teasing the rest of us every chance she got. But nobody minded. She's really funny. For instance, she's the one who came up with my nickname. When Lola heard I was African American, White, Japanese, and Korean, she said my name shouldn't be Amy Hodges—it should be Amy Hodgepodge. Some of my friends are multiracial, too. Lola and Cole are African American and White. But Lola says nobody is as mixed as me.

"The lecture *was* way cool," Rusty agreed. "But it's too bad our teachers had to ruin it by turning it into a class assignment."

"Don't be silly," I told him. "Coming up with a green project will be fun."

"A school assignment, fun? Are you crazy, Amy?" Jesse exclaimed.

Lola laughed. "Be nice to Amy, you guys," she

joked. "She's still kind of new to this whole school thing, remember?"

I laughed along with my friends. As usual, Lola was only kidding around. Besides, she was right. I'd only been at Emerson Charter School since earlier that year. Before that, I was homeschooled by my parents and grandparents. When we moved to Maple Heights, I asked them if I could try going to regular school. I was glad I did. Emerson was great because it didn't just have regular classes like reading and math. We also had art or music class every day, plus tons of lectures, field trips, and other special events. And the best bonus of all was that I had made lots of good friends.

"Anyway, I think Amy's right," Maya spoke up in her soft, sweet way. "It could be really interesting to see what each class comes up with for its green project."

The fourth grade at Emerson is divided into two sections. Lola, Pia, Rusty, and I are in Mrs. Clark's class along with a bunch of other kids.

Jesse, Maya, Cole, and everyone else have Mrs. Musgrove. After the lecture, each teacher had given her class an assignment to come up with ideas for a green class project. We had until Monday to think of something. Today was Friday, so that didn't give us much time.

Just then Cole came hurrying over. "I was just talking to Spencer in line," he said as he set down his tray. "You should hear his idea for the class project. He wants to make a compost pile in the back of Mrs. Clark's classroom. Can you believe it? He says we could throw everything on

there, like lunch leftovers, old test papers, and leaves and grass and stuff from outside. He says we could even use whatever the first-graders clean out of their hamster cages."

"Ew!" Pia wrinkled her nose. "A compost pile right in our classroom? I don't think so!"

"It figures Spencer would come up with something like that," Jesse said. "He's gross."

That wasn't very nice, but I knew what she meant. Spencer loved playing outside and never seemed to mind when he got all dirty. He especially liked things that other people thought

were icky. Once he even ate a stepped-on french fry just because Rory Fuwicki dared him to.

"Well, composting *is* green," Lola said. "Our grandma has a big compost pile, and she says it helps her garden grow."

"Yeah, but Nana's compost pile is in her backyard, not inside her house," Cole pointed out.

Jesse nodded. "I think we can come up with a better idea than that."

"Or at least a less stinky one!" Pia added.

"How about building a windmill?" Rusty suggested. "We could try to get it to power the classroom lights or something."

Maya looked doubtful. "Sounds kind of complicated and probably expensive," she said, reaching for her milk. "I think it's supposed to be something we can do all by ourselves."

"Yeah, we're not scientists," Lola said. "But wait, I have an idea. What if we wrote a song about the environment and sang it at our next school concert?"

Jesse wrinkled her nose. "You always want

to do songs," she complained. "We should do something different."

Jesse could be a little too bossy sometimes. She always thinks her opinion is the best one. Still, this time nobody argued with Jesse—not even Lola.

"You're right," Lola said instead. "Being green is really important. We need to come up with something really great."

Pia popped a grape into her mouth. "What do you think, Amy? You're being kind of quiet."

"Maybe she's just thinking extra hard to come up with a fabulous idea," Maya said. "You know, like the one she had for the art contest."

I smiled sheepishly. "Sorry," I said. "Actually I was just trying to figure out how many hours are left until my Grandma Hodges gets here tomorrow."

"Oh, right!" Maya nodded. "I almost forgot your grandma is coming to visit. You must be so excited."

"I am," I said with a happy sigh. "I haven't

seen Grandma Hodges in such a long time!"

My dad's parents live in Wilkerson—a town almost three hundred miles away.

"Is your grandfather coming with her?" Rusty asked.

I shook my head sadly. "He can't come this time," I said. "He already agreed to go to a reunion with some old friends from the Navy. But he did promise to visit soon."

I was a little sad that Grandpa Hodges wouldn't be coming. But at least Grandma Hodges was still coming. I couldn't wait to see her!

Chapter 2

It was Saturday morning. Obaasan, Lola, my dog Giggles, and I were walking through the local Farmers' Market. I had been there a few times before, and I loved it. People came from all around the city to sell their fresh fruits and vegetables, flowers, baked goods, organic honey, local handicrafts, and all sorts of other great things. It was so popular that the closest parking spot we'd been able to find was five blocks away.

"I bet Grandma Hodges would love this. We should have waited for her to get here so she could come, too."

Obaasan looked over at me. Obaasan means grandmother in Japanese. It's what I call my other grandmother because she's from Japan. She lives with us, along with my grandpa. He's from Korea, so I call him Harabujy.

"Yes, but the reason we're here is to pick up some fresh flowers and dinner ingredients for her visit," Obaasan reminded me. "Your mother and I want to fix a special dinner for her first night here."

Lola laughed. "Hey, wait a minute," she said. "I thought the reason we were here was to get some Dyver City Daffy Taffy."

"That's the reason *you're* here," I said with a giggle. Lola had gone to the Farmers' Market with her family a couple of weekends earlier.

She had found a brand-new booth that sold locally made taffy. Ever since then, she'd been telling us all how delicious it was. I'd asked if she could come along that morning just so she could show me the new booth.

"Just wait until you try this taffy, Amy." Lola licked her lips. "It's the best!"

"I wonder if Giggles will like it," I said, glancing down at my dog. Giggles was the cutest, sweetest terrier mix in the world. When he heard me say his name, he looked up and barked. Then he went back to trying to pull me along faster at the end of his leash. He was staring around and sniffing at everything we passed. His stubby little tail wagged nonstop.

Obaasan shook her head. "I suggest you don't try to find out," she warned. "Do you not remember what happened when you fed him those cherry candies, Amy?"

"What happened?" Lola asked.

I grimaced. "Uh, let's just say that what happened wasn't very pretty!" I said. "Poor

Giggles! I guess he doesn't like cherries."

Just then, Giggles started barking at some teenage boys passing by.

"Shhh, Giggles," Lola said. "It's not nice to bark at people."

"He's just excited to be here." I reached down and picked up Giggles for a hug. He tried to lick my face, but I quickly moved out of the way. He might be the sweetest dog that ever lived, but his breath sure wasn't. Then he started wriggling and tried to jump down. For a second, his leash got looped around my arm.

"Careful with that leash, Little Mitsukai," Obaasan said. That's her nickname for me. It means "Little Angel" in Japanese. "It's very crowded here. You'll have to watch that his leash doesn't get tangled around people's legs."

"It would be a lot easier if I could just take it off," I said, straightening out the leash. "He always stays close when I let him off his leash at home or in Lola's yard or at the dog park."

Obaasan shook her head. "You heard what

your mother said before we left home. He needs to stay on his leash today. There are far too many people here for Giggles to be wandering around loose. Besides, we should be considerate of the other shoppers."

I nodded. But secretly I didn't really see how it would be inconsiderate. Giggles was so cute and friendly that I was sure the other shoppers would love to meet him. Besides, it seemed kind of inconsiderate to Giggles to make him stay on his leash when he'd rather run around and explore. But I didn't say any of that out loud.

Meanwhile Lola was pointing to the other end of the crowded market. "There's the taffy stand," she said, pointing. "Over by the jams and jellies table." Lola made her eyes go really wide and started rocking back and forth like she was in some kind of trance. "Taffy, taffy. Must have taffy," she said as if she were a zombie. I cracked up laughing.

Obaasan checked her watch. "We're already running a bit late since it took so long to park," she said. "Why don't you girls go ahead and buy your taffy while I pick up the flowers and vegetables? I'll meet you over by the taffy stand when I'm finished. Just be sure to stay together, and keep a close eye on Giggles."

"Okay," I said. "We'll see you in a few minutes."

Obaasan hurried off toward a big flower stand, while Lola and I headed for the taffy stand. It was slow going, since the Farmers' Market was pretty crowded. Along the way, we passed a bakery with a huge stack of delicious-looking brownies set out on a small, round table in front.

"If I don't like the taffy, maybe I'll come here and try some of those brownies," I said.

"There's no way you won't love this taffy," Lola promised. "It's the best, I swear. It'll make brownies taste like spinach and lima beans."

"Really?" I said with a smile. "I kind of like lima beans." That made us both start laughing.

Next we passed a table selling potted

houseplants. It was so crowded with plants that it looked like a mini jungle.

"Everything here is so green," I said. "You know—just like our lecture yesterday. I wonder what we'll end up doing for our class project." We'd talked about the project all through lunch and on the bus after school the day before. But we hadn't come up with any really great ideas yet.

"Too bad we can't have our own Farmers' Market at Emerson," Lola said. "If only we could grow all these fruits and vegetables and stuff in the parking lot!"

I giggled at the thought. "Maybe we could use Spencer's compost idea and grow them right in our classroom!"

Just then Giggles barked and leaped forward. The sudden move almost pulled the leash out of my hand.

"Calm down, Giggles!" I cried. "You're going to yank my arm off!"

Giggles didn't pay any attention. He strained

at the end of his leash, whining at something.

"Looks like he wants to play with that dog."
Lola pointed to another dog that was playing
with a stick nearby. "Or maybe he's just jealous
because that dog doesn't have to stay on a leash."

The other dog was a pretty, medium-sized
dog with silky fur. She trotted toward us, her
tail wagging cheerfully. Giggles barked, his tail
wagging, too. The two of them sniffed noses,
then started playing together.

"Aw, they do want to play." I bit my lip,
glancing around to make sure Obaasan was
nowhere in sight. "Maybe I'll let him off the
leash . . . just for a little while."

"Are you sure?" Lola asked.

"It'll be okay. He just wants to say hi to
his new friend." I bent down and unclipped
the leash from his collar. "Be good, Giggles," I
whispered into his fuzzy ear. "I'll be back in a
minute."

Giggles barked happily. As soon as the
leash was off, he raced around the other dog in

❀ 16 ❀

circles. She jumped up and spun around. Soon
the two of them were chasing each other and
having a great time.

"Come on," I said. "We'd better hurry. It looks
like there's a long line at the taffy stand. We'll
just keep an eye on him from there."

We hurried over and took our place at the end
of the line. "Don't worry, it's worth the wait," Lola
said. "Besides, that gives us time to decide what
flavors to get." She pointed to a big whiteboard
hanging over the stand. There were at least two
dozen flavors listed on it.

"Wow!" I said. "You weren't kidding when you
said they had a lot of flavors."

"I know. My favorite so far is coconut. But
today I think I'll try the root beer flavor."

"Root beer? That sounds awesome!" I stood on my tiptoes for a better look at the sign. "Berry swirl sounds good, too. Ooh! And so does apricot cream."

Lola laughed. "That's the only bad thing about this taffy," she said. "It's too hard to decide which kind to get!"

We talked about the flavors until we finally got to the front of the line. By then, I'd decided to get berry swirl and sour apple. Lola picked root beer and chocolate mint.

"Come on," Lola said as soon as we'd paid for our taffy. "Let's sit down over there and do a taste test. Your grandma won't be able to miss us. That bench is right near the taffy stand."

"Okay. Just let me put Giggles back on his leash before Obaasan comes to meet us."

Lola and I both looked over to where we'd left Giggles and his new friend.

"Wait! Where is he?" Lola asked.

I quickly stood up and looked around. "Oh no!" I cried. Giggles was nowhere in sight!

Chapter 3

"Giggles?" I called, rushing over to the spot where I'd left him. "Giggles, come! Here, boy!"

"Here, Giggles!" Lola added. She let out a loud whistle. "Where are you?"

I felt my heart start to pound as I turned around in circles. There were tons of people

everywhere around us. There were even some dogs. A young man was walking a yellow lab puppy. A tiny black dog was cuddled in a woman's arms.

But there was no sign of Giggles's honey-brown fur. I couldn't find his new friend, either. Where had they gone?

"Don't panic," Lola said. "I'm sure he's around here somewhere. He probably went over to the hot dog stand to beg for food."

"You're probably right," I said. "He loves hot dogs. Come on, let's check."

We raced over to the snack stand. But Giggles wasn't there, either. He also wasn't at either of the bakery stands. Or hiding behind the portable restrooms. Or anywhere else.

We were searching the plant stand when we ran into Obaasan. By then I was sick with panic. We told her what had happened.

"You let him off the leash?!" Obaasan asked in surprise.

Tears welled up in my eyes. "I'm sorry,

Obaasan," I said. "I know you told me not to. And now I really, really wish I'd listened to you!"

"We'll talk about that later." Obaasan put her arm around my shoulders. "First, let's find Giggles."

Lola reached over and squeezed my hand. "Don't worry, Amy. He's got to be around here somewhere, right?"

Even though we searched like crazy for the next half hour, Giggles was nowhere to be found. Finally Obaasan sighed, checked her watch, and shook her head.

"I'm afraid we'd better head home, girls," she said. "It's getting late."

"But we can't leave him!" I exclaimed, heartbroken at the thought of leaving without my best friend. "He doesn't know how to get home from here. What if I never see him again?" I burst into tears.

Obaasan shook her head. "Try not to worry, Little Mitsukai," she said gently. "Remember what I always say—you need to think positively.

Giggles is wearing his collar, yes?"

I sniffled and nodded. "I only took off his leash, not his collar," I said, holding up the leash.

"Good. That means he's wearing his tag with our phone number on it." Obaasan smiled. "Surely someone will find him and call."

"That's right, Amy." Lola gasped and clapped her hands excitedly. "In fact, maybe that's why we can't find him. Maybe someone already took him in and called your folks, and he's waiting for us at home right now!"

That idea made me feel a tiny bit better. We hurried to the car and headed for home, dropping Lola off on the way.

When we got home, I raced inside. "Did anyone call?" I asked. "Did you hear anything about Giggles?"

"Giggles?" my dad said. He was in the kitchen cutting some carrots into small slices. "What was that about Giggles calling? Did he learn to use the phone?"

Normally I laugh at my dad's silly jokes. But

today it just didn't seem funny. I stared at my mom, who had just stepped in from the laundry room holding some dish towels.

"Did anyone call to say they found Giggles?" I repeated urgently.

"What are you talking about?" she asked.

With Obaasan's help, I told her what had happened. Mom started to frown as soon as she heard about me taking off his leash. By the time I finished explaining, her frown had deepened.

"This is exactly why I told you not to let him off the leash," she said sternly. "We don't make up these rules for no reason, Amy. It's because we know something like this could happen. I thought you understood that you had a responsibility to keep Giggles on the leash, and I'm very disappointed that you disobeyed."

My eyes welled up with tears. I knew I'd made a mistake. But hearing Mom say it made me feel even worse than I already did.

"I'm sorry," I whispered as tears spilled onto my cheeks.

Meanwhile my dad stood up and stepped over to the phone hanging on the kitchen wall. "To start with, I'll call the local animal shelters," he said, grabbing the phone book from a nearby drawer. "We'll see if anyone has turned in a dog matching Giggles's description."

I watched as he dialed the first number. I was trying to think positively, like Obaasan had said. But it wasn't easy.

Soon Dad had called all the shelters listed in the phone book. None of them had Giggles.

"I left our number," he said as he hung up from the last call. "They'll let us know if he shows up."

At that moment the doorbell chimed. "That must be Grandma Hodges," my mom said, checking her watch. "She's right on time."

"I'll get it!" Dad hurried toward the front door.

Mom and Obaasan followed, and I drifted along after them. My mom's dad, Harabujy, was also heading for the front door.

"That must be Ella," he said.

My dad flung open the front door. "Mama!" he cried happily.

"Son!" Grandma Hodges bustled in and grabbed him by the shoulders, looking him up and down. "You're so skinny. Looks like you could hang glide on a potato chip. What's that wife of yours feeding you? Air sandwiches?" She turned to my mother and winked. "Hello, Soo. I'm gonna have to help you fatten this boy up before I go."

Mom laughed and reached out for a hug. "Be my guest. The kitchen's all yours, Ella. It's good to see you!"

"Ah, that's what they all say," Grandma Hodges exclaimed, hugging her back.

She looked just the same as I remembered. She's tall and beautiful and soft to hug. Her hair was an amazing silver color and she wore it in twists. Her black eyes were always twinkling—

especially when she cracked one of her jokes, which was often. I guess that's where my dad got his humor from. She made me laugh so hard sometimes that my stomach hurt. She's also very stylish and always wore interesting and colorful clothes and jewelry. Pia would love her. They could trade fashion tips.

"And where's my Amy?" Grandma Hodges asked as my dad stepped outside to get her bags. "I need to see my beautiful girl!"

"I'm here, Grandma," I said weakly, stepping forward.

She put her hand to her heart and widened her eyes. "Look at you!" she cried. "Last time I saw something that pretty, I was looking in the mirror!" she said, laughing.

Ordinarily, I'd laugh at her joke, but I wasn't in the mood. Grandma Hodges took a hard look at me. "What's with the long face, baby?"

"I'm afraid we've had a difficult morning," Mom spoke up. "Giggles is lost."

"Goodness gracious!" Grandma Hodges looked horrified. "Well, I can see why you'd be upset. What happened?"

Once again I told the story, with Obaasan helping. Grandma Hodges shook her head through the whole thing. But she didn't scold me for letting him off the leash.

"Well," she said. "I'm sure Obaasan is right, and Giggles will soon be safely home again. Try not to worry your pretty head about it, baby. Here, I know what might take your mind off your troubles . . ."

She turned and rummaged in one of the suitcases my dad had just carried in. It turned out she'd brought me several gifts—a hand-knit scarf, some books, and a few other fun things.

The gifts were really nice. Normally I would

have been excited about them—and about seeing Grandma Hodges, of course. But all I could do right then was pretend to be excited. Because the truth was, the only gift I wanted was to have Giggles back home again.

The rest of that afternoon and evening were probably the worst of my entire life. I could barely eat the delicious dinner Obaasan made for Grandma Hodges's arrival. My mind kept wandering as everyone else chatted, catching up on all the family news. Even looking at the photo album Grandma Hodges had brought with pictures of her and Grandpa Hodges didn't distract me from worrying about Giggles.

I excused myself as soon as I could and went up to my room. Heading straight for my bookcase, I pulled out my scrapbook.

Scrapbooking is my favorite hobby. It all started when Obaasan gave me some pretty handmade paper. Ever since, I've kept track of all the special people and times in my life in my scrapbook.

Giggles has his own set of pages near the front. There are pictures of him as a puppy, some of him at our old house, one from the time I dressed him up in a tuxedo and top hat for Halloween, and lots more. He's also in plenty of the photos on the other pages. I flipped through, looking at every single one. Would I ever get to see the real Giggles again? Or would these photos be all I had left from now on?

That thought was too terrible to bear. I closed the scrapbook and put it away. Even though

it wasn't anywhere near my usual bedtime, I decided to go to bed. Maybe when I woke up in the morning, my parents would tell me that someone had called while I was asleep to say that Giggles was safe.

I put on my pajamas and crawled into bed. It felt strange not having his familiar fuzzy little body right next to me. I even missed the smell of his stinky breath. I should've let him lick my face this morning when he tried. I ended up tossing and turning for hours. Every time I was about to fall asleep, I'd think about Giggles and wake up again, feeling sad. If only I hadn't let him off his leash! This was all my fault . . .

I guess I finally fell asleep sometime after midnight, because the next thing I knew, I woke up to find the sun shining through my windows.

"Giggles?!" I blurted out, glancing around the room. I was hoping it had all been a bad dream and that he would be right there snoozing away on my bed. But I knew in my heart that wasn't going to happen.

Jumping out of bed, I pulled on my slippers. Then I raced for the stairs. It was after eight o'clock—I couldn't believe I'd slept so late after being so worried.

"Did anyone call about Giggles?" I asked as I burst into the kitchen. My parents, Grandma Hodges, and Harabujy were all sitting around the table as Obaasan fiddled with the teakettle nearby.

The adults all exchanged a look. "Sorry, Amy," Mom said. "No calls yet."

Chapter 4

"Don't fret, child." Grandma Hodges poured more orange juice into my glass even though I'd only drunk a few sips so far. "After breakfast, I'll take you out and help you put up lost dog signs around the neighborhood, all right? That way we'll get the whole community involved in tracking down little Giggles."

I smiled weakly. Grandma Hodges loved to talk about the community and stuff like that. She did a lot of work as a community organizer.

"Thanks," I said. I could even use one of the photos from my scrapbook on the flyer. I hoped the signs would help. But I wasn't too sure.

A little while later, Mom, Dad, and Harabujy went upstairs to get showered and dressed. Grandma Hodges was still sitting at the table sipping a cup of coffee. Obaasan was at the stove.

She'd just served me a plate of scrambled eggs. I just kept staring at the phone, hoping it would ring.

"Stop staring at that phone, baby. A watched pot never boils," warned Grandma Hodges.

Obaasan turned around with the spatula in her hand. "Yes, try not to worry, Little Mitsukai," she said. "It is still early—barely nine o'clock. Stay positive."

"I'm trying." I pushed my eggs around on the plate. My stomach felt funny, and I definitely didn't feel like eating.

Just then the phone rang. I jumped so high I almost fell off my chair.

"Good morning, Hodges residence," Obaasan said when she answered the phone. Then she listened for a moment, and smiled. "Oh, thank you! That's wonderful news!"

"Is it about Giggles?" I asked, my heart in my throat.

She nodded, smiling. Then she covered the phone with her hand. "A gentleman found him

last night," she said. "Giggles is safe and sound at his apartment."

Less than half an hour later, I was in the car with Dad and Grandma Hodges. We were driving through the city, following the directions Obaasan had taken down.

"I think we're almost there," Dad said, peering out at the street signs. "This makes sense. We're not too far from the Farmers' Market."

Not long after we passed the Farmers' Market, the neighborhood started to change. This part of town was pretty run-down. There was graffiti on some of the buildings, weeds grew out of big cracks in the sidewalk, and many of the houses' windows were broken.

Grandma Hodges was holding the directions. "Says here we're supposed to meet this fella at his garden," she said. "Look. That's it over there!"

My dad looked where she was pointing. I leaned forward as much as my seat belt would let me. Just ahead was a big empty lot between two brick buildings. A rusty chain link fence with vines growing on it blocked it off from the sidewalk. The gate was open, and I spotted a slightly stooped man inside. Beside him were . . . two playful dogs!

"Giggles!" I shouted. "There he is! Pull over, Dad, pull over!"

I could hardly stand to wait as my dad parked the car. After a moment I was finally able to open the door and rush outside.

"Giggles! Here, boy!" I yelled.

Giggles heard me. He barked, then raced out to meet me.

"Giggles!" I grabbed him and hugged him tight. Tears were streaming down my face, but I didn't care. I was just so happy to have him back!

"Looks like he recognizes you, all right!"

I glanced up and saw the man smiling down at me. Close up, I could see that he was pretty old—older than any of my grandparents. He had a kind, wrinkled face. He was wearing faded

overalls and a battered sun hat.

By now Dad and Grandma Hodges had hurried to join me. "You must be Mr. Coleman," my dad said, sticking out his hand. "Thanks so much for calling us about Giggles."

"It was my pleasure." The man shook his hand. "But please, call me Irving."

Dad and Grandma Hodges introduced themselves and me. I put on Giggles's leash and stood up.

"Thank you so much," I told Irving, wiping away my tears with one hand while keeping a tight hold on Giggles's leash with the other. "I'm so glad you found Giggles."

"Didn't so much find him," Irving replied with a chuckle. "More like he found me. Or rather, Babe there found him and brought him to me." He gestured to his dog, who was sniffing curiously at the edge of Grandma Hodges's skirt. "Brought her with me to the Farmers' Market yesterday when I dropped off some vegetables, and she managed to slip off her leash. Figured she'd run on home, since it isn't far. But I didn't expect she'd bring a friend with her!"

My dad laughed. "Well, we're certainly glad she did," he said, leaning down to scratch Babe's silky ears.

"Wanted to call right away, but it was pretty late by the time they turned up," Irving said. "Hope you didn't worry too much, Amy."

Now that I had Giggles back, all my worry had already faded away. "It's okay," I said. "Anyway, it's my fault I had to worry. I shouldn't have let Giggles off his leash in the first place."

"True enough." Irving nodded. "Good lesson to learn, though it's a shame it had to be the hard way, eh?"

I smiled. "Yeah. But I definitely won't do it again!"

Grandma Hodges was peering over the fence. "Is this where you grow the vegetables you mentioned?" she asked. "Looks like you've got the makings of a fine community garden here."

Irving sighed and rubbed his face. "Yep, that's

what it used to be," he said. "Was a beautiful place once. Bunch of us started it about fifteen years ago now. Kept people in fresh produce for blocks around. But I'm the only one left out of the original group." He shook his head and took off his hat. "Now I'm just about out of funds and manpower. Been trying to raise a little cash selling produce at the Farmers' Market, but it's not enough. Not sure I'll be able to keep it going past this season."

"Goodness gracious," Grandma Hodges shook her head. "What a shame."

I agreed. The garden was overgrown and a bit run-down, but there were also tidy rows of tomato plants and peppers and lettuce, cucumbers, lots of pretty flowers, and more.

A few minutes later we said good-bye to Irving and headed home. I sat in the backseat with Giggles in my lap listening to Grandma Hodges talk about Irving's garden.

"It's an outrage," she exclaimed. "How can a whole community be so apathetic toward what could be a beautiful addition to their own neighborhood? It's shameful! Why, if I was going to be in town more than a week, I'd be doing something about it, that's for certain!"

My dad chuckled. "I'm sure you would, Mama," he said. "You never saw a problem you didn't try to fix."

"That's right. And it's a good thing, too. Or you'd still have your big toe stuck in the bathtub faucet!" she exclaimed.

"What?" I asked, laughing.

"Yeah, your father was a handful when he was a youngster. If I turned my back for two seconds, he was into some mischief. Now, back to that garden. It wouldn't take much to fix it up, either," Grandma Hodges mused. "All it needs is a few people getting off their rusty, dusty behinds to do their part. The hard part is convincing them how important it is to give back to the community. You'd think they'd be convinced just by walking by and seeing all that beautiful green space in the middle of the city."

She continued talking, but I hardly heard. I'd just had a great idea.

"Hey!" I cried. "That's it!"

Dad glanced at me in the rearview mirror. "What's it?" he asked.

"Irving's garden," I exclaimed. "What if my fourth-grade class helped Irving fix it up as our green project?"

"Green project?" Grandma Hodges asked.

I quickly explained the class project. "We

could spend a weekend helping him weed and plant and stuff," I said excitedly. "After all, you can't get much greener than a garden! And then when everyone in the neighborhood sees how beautiful it could be, they'll definitely want to help keep it going!"

"Sounds like a good idea, Amy," my dad said.

Grandma Hodges clapped her hands. "Brilliant!" she exclaimed. "It's absolutely perfect, baby. I knew you must have inherited some of my activist spirit!"

I laughed. That made Giggles bark. I grabbed him and hugged him. At least one good thing had come out of almost losing him—I'd come up with the perfect idea for our project!

Chapter 5

"So what do you think?" I held my breath and looked around at my friends. It was Monday morning, and we were standing in the school hallway. I'd just told them about my idea to make Irving's community garden our green project.

Lola clapped her hands. "It's an awesome idea!" she cried. "Let's do it!"

Jesse nodded. "You should tell Mrs. Clark right away."

"Definitely!" Pia added as Maya nodded eagerly.

"Okay." I grinned. I wasn't sure if my friends were going to love the idea as much as I did. I knew it was silly, but I always worried that they would think my ideas were dumb. It was such a relief to hear them say they liked it. As soon as Mrs. Clark walked into homeroom, I raised my hand and told her the idea. The rest of the class listened, too.

"A community garden?" Jennifer Higgins said. She wrinkled her nose. "That sounds lame . . . and messy."

Her response was no surprise. Jennifer doesn't like any idea she didn't think of herself.

"Are you kidding?" Lola cried. "It's an awesome idea! What could be greener than a garden?"

"I agree. It's an excellent idea, Amy." Mrs. Clark looked around the room. "Does anyone else agree?"

Almost everyone cheered and raised their hands. Rusty raised both hands. Finally even Jennifer slowly raised her hand.

"I guess it could be okay," she said. "My grandparents have a big garden on their horse farm and it's pretty cool."

As soon as she said that, her friend Liza raised her hand, too. She does everything Jennifer does and likes everything Jennifer likes. So does their other best friend, Gracie. But Gracie was in Mrs. Musgrove's class and wouldn't be working with us.

"It's unanimous then," Mrs. Clark said. "And actually, this is such a wonderful idea that I think I'll see if Mrs. Musgrove's students want to join us in one big project instead of each class doing a separate one. What do you think?"

Everyone cheered again. I joined in. This was going to be great!

❀ ❀ ❀

After Mrs. Musgrove and her class agreed that helping Irving was a great idea, Mrs. Clark called to let him know the good news. After lunch that day, the whole fourth grade piled into Mrs. Clark's class for a planning meeting. I couldn't believe how quickly all of this was coming together!

"The first thing we should talk about is a fund-raiser," Mrs. Clark began.

"Why?" Rusty called out. "I thought we were fixing up a garden, not buying one!"

A few people laughed. Mrs. Musgrove frowned at Rusty, but Mrs. Clark just smiled.

"We'll need to raise funds to pay for the tools and materials you'll need to fix it up," she explained.

"Oh! I get it." Rusty slunk down in his seat.

"We can hold our fund-raiser this weekend right here at Emerson, then go fix up the garden the following weekend," Mrs. Clark said. "So now we just have to figure out what to do for the fund-raiser. Any ideas?"

I couldn't help feeling a little let down. I'd
been looking forward to getting to work on
Irving's garden right away. But Mrs. Clark's plan
made sense. We could do a much better job if we
had enough money to buy everything we needed.
So I started trying to think of fund-raising ideas.

"I know!" Jennifer's friend Gracie called out.
"How about selling scented candles?"

"We just did that last spring," Cole said. "My
mom said she never wants to see a candle again."

Several people laughed. "Mine, too!" Pia
agreed. "Or smell one, either."

I hadn't been at Emerson when they did
the candle fund-raiser. But I was still glad we
weren't going to do that. It didn't sound very
interesting.

"What about a charity basketball
tournament?" Evelyn suggested, waving her
hand in the air. Evelyn loves sports.

"That could work," Mrs. Clark agreed. "What
does everyone think?"

Most people shrugged. Yasmin, a really smart

Iranian girl with glasses, said, "Sounds kind of boring." Then she glanced over. "Sorry, Evelyn."

"Shouldn't we do something that goes along with the green theme?" Lola asked.

A bunch of students nodded. "Maybe we could sell organic coffee," Angela said. "My dad loves that stuff."

"Or we could sell those long-life light bulbs," Stanley called out.

Lola shook her head. "None of these ideas seem quite right," she said. "Maybe it doesn't have to be another green idea after all."

Thinking about green ideas reminded me of the Farmers' Market. And that reminded me of all the delicious-looking baked goods I'd seen there. "Hey, maybe we should do a bake sale!" I exclaimed.

"I know!" Jesse cried at the same time. "Let's have a car wash!"

"Ooh, a bake sale would be fun," Angela said. "I bet my aunt would help me make some of her special raspberry chiffon pie."

"No way, I think Jesse's car wash idea would be better," Jackie said. "My cousin had one at his school, and they raised a ton of money."

"Yeah, and I'd rather wash cars than bake chiffon pies," Rory called out with a laugh.

Several other kids were also calling out comments. Some agreed with Rory and Jackie. Others supported my bake sale idea. Everyone

seemed to be taking sides.

Soon everyone was squabbling. Finally Mrs. Musgrove clapped her hands. "Enough!" she said sternly.

Mrs. Clark nodded. "It sounds like there's strong interest for each of these ideas," she said. "So why don't we do both? You can split into two teams. One group can organize the car wash, and the other can do the bake sale." She pointed to me and Jesse. "And I know the perfect students to be your team leaders!"

Chapter 6

Being a team leader for the bake sale was a little scary. It seemed like a huge task to organize an entire bake sale in less than a week!

But I knew I would have lots of help from my team which included Lola, Pia, Angela, Spencer, Cole, Rusty, and to my surprise, Jennifer, Liza, and Gracie. I had expected Cole and Rusty to do the car wash, too, but they both wanted to be in my group. "We get to taste-test all the cookies and stuff, right?" Rusty said, licking his lips.

Maya decided to help out with Jesse's car wash along with Rory, Danny, Yasmin, Jackie, Evelyn, and Stanley.

"I like both ideas," Maya told me with her sweet smile. "But I'm not a very good baker. I always get the sugar and the salt mixed up."

"Yikes. Maybe you are better off washing cars

instead," Lola said jokingly.

Everyone seemed so excited about our project that I couldn't help being excited, too.

The only person more excited about the project than me was Grandma Hodges. I told her and Obaasan all about it right after school. They were sitting in the kitchen drinking tea together when I got home.

"It's so wonderful to see you getting involved in good causes, Amy!" Grandma Hodges exclaimed, hugging me so hard that I winced.

"You're just like your old grandma! Now, what are you going to do first?"

"I'm not sure," I said, feeling nervous again. "I've never done anything like this before. Especially not as the leader of a group."

"You can do it, Amy," Obaasan said. "Think positively!"

"She's right," Grandma Hodges agreed. "But you've got more than positive thinking working for you this time, pretty girl. You've got me! This kind of thing is right up my alley."

"You mean you'll help me with the bake sale?" I grinned at her hopefully. "That would be awesome!"

"Just try to stop me! And you know my baked goods are so scrumptious, they'll have your customers drooling like Giggles on a hot summer day," she said with a laugh. "Now, let's get busy—you don't have much time. There's a lot to think about beyond baked goods, you know."

"Like what?" I asked.

She started ticking things off on her fingers.

"You'll need to arrange for tables to put your baked goods on, bags for the customers to carry things away in, napkins, perhaps forks . . ."

Obaasan stood up. "Why don't I make us some more tea?"

"Thanks," I said, though I wasn't really thinking about tea. There were too many other things to think about! "Wow," I told Grandma Hodges. "I already knew putting on a bake sale was going to be kind of complicated. But it's even more complicated than I thought!"

She chuckled. "Don't be alarmed," she said. "I know you can do it. After all, you're *my* granddaughter!"

I grinned. "That's true," I said. "And I'm definitely glad you're here to save the day! Do you think some of your community organizing expertise can rub off on me?"

"I know it can, Amy," she declared. "You just need three things."

"Cakes, pies, and cookies?" I guessed.

She laughed again. "Well, those, too," she

agreed. "But I was talking about three different things. You need to plan carefully, you have to be willing to be flexible, and most of all, you need to have a sense of humor!"

The next day in art class, both groups made posters to advertise our fund-raisers. We hung some up around school and outside in the parking lot. Then we divided up the rest of the posters to take home and put up around our neighborhoods. Some kids even volunteered to have their parents take posters to their offices all around the city.

That afternoon we had another planning meeting. The bake sale group met in Mrs. Clark's room, and the car wash students went over to Mrs. Musgrove's.

Everyone was pretty excited. The room was abuzz with talking and laughter as everyone sat down. I glanced at Mrs. Clark, waiting for her to take charge of the meeting.

She smiled back at me. "Go ahead, Amy," she

said. "This is your meeting. I'll be right here at my desk grading papers if you need anything."

I gulped as she sat down at her desk. I was supposed to run the meeting all by myself?! I'd never done anything like that before. I wasn't that good at speaking in front of crowds. I could feel myself starting to sweat. Then I thought about Irving and how great it was going to be to make his garden beautiful again. That made me feel a bit braver.

In a low voice, I said, "Hello, everyone. Thanks

for giving me your attention." But nobody was listening to me. They were all talking amongst themselves. I started to chicken out and go back to my seat, but Mrs. Clark shot me an encouraging look. So I took a deep breath and

spoke up really loudly. "Quiet down, everyone!" I called out. "Please? We need to get started." My voice was shaky, but it did the trick. Everyone quieted down.

Then I cleared my throat, trying to figure out what to say next. I thought back over everything Grandma Hodges and I had talked about the evening before. She'd also helped me make a couple of lists.

"There's a lot to do before the sale this weekend." I started to forget my nervousness as I talked. "First, we need a lot of stuff to set up with. So let's figure out who can bring what."

I read out the list of things Grandma Hodges and I had come up with. Evelyn's father had a couple of folding tables he used at the monthly flea market, so she volunteered to bring those. A couple of other kids had more tables and chairs they could bring. Different people agreed to take care of the shopping bags, tablecloths, and the rest. Mrs. Clark even offered to talk to the school cafeteria about supplying napkins and forks and stuff.

"Okay, next comes the fun part—the baked goods!" I said after I'd checked off the last thing on the supply list.

Everyone cheered. "Now we're talking!" Rusty exclaimed.

I pulled out my other list. "I tried to divide things up so we'd have a good variety of baked goods," I said. "Angela, can you make a few of those raspberry chiffon pies you were talking about yesterday?"

"Definitely," Angela agreed. "I already called my aunt for the recipe."

"Jennifer, Liza, Gracie—I thought you could make brownies—maybe some chocolate ones and some butterscotch ones, too?"

Jennifer shook her head and raised her hand. "I have a much better idea," she said. "My aunt has a great recipe." She shot a smug look toward Angela. "It's her top-secret recipe for pineapple upside-down cake. We'll bring that instead."

"Yeah, I've tasted it," Liza added. "It's fabulous!"

I frowned and looked down at my list. This wasn't going the way I'd planned. I had figured they would agree to bring the brownies. Now what? Then I heard Grandma Hodges's voice inside my head: *You have to be flexible*, it said.

"Okay," I told Jennifer and her friends. "I guess that would be fine."

Luckily, everybody else agreed to bake the stuff I assigned to them. "Maybe we can get together at someone's house on Friday and do some of the baking together," Angela suggested.

"That's a good idea," I said. "I'm sure my parents would let us do some of it at my house. That way my grandma could help. She's a great baker."

"Ooh, you mean your Obaasan?" Pia said. "Yeah, she makes those awesome rice crackers!"

I shook my head. "Not her—my Grandma Hodges is visiting this week, remember? She makes these super yummy, double chocolate chip cookies."

"Wow, it sounds like we're going to have tons of great food," Pia exclaimed. "We're totally going to beat the pants off of the car wash team!"

"Yeah!" Cole cheered.

Most of the other kids laughed and cheered, too. I was kind of surprised. They all seemed to think we were competing against the car washers. I hadn't really thought about it that way. It felt kind of weird to be competing against Jesse and Maya and the rest of the kids on that team.

But I tried not to think of it that way. The important thing was that both teams raised lots of money for Irving's garden. I just had to stay focused on that.

Chapter 7

That Friday afternoon, Lola, Pia, Rusty, Cole, Angela, and Spencer gathered at my house for our baking session. By the time everyone got there, the kitchen was pretty crowded! Jennifer and her friends didn't come, saying that they'd rather work at her house. Somehow that didn't surprise me.

"This is so cool. I've never tried to cook anything more complicated than toast!" said Angela.

"Yeah," Rusty admitted. "I don't think I'll be very good at baking, either. The only bakin' I'm used to is the kind that's served with eggs."

Spencer laughed. "I'm great at *eating* cakes and cookies," he bragged. "I don't know about *making* them, though."

"Don't worry. My Grandma Hodges is a great baker. She promised to help us."

"Did I hear my name?" Grandma Hodges hurried into the room, followed by my mom and Obaasan. "Here I am! Who's ready to start baking?"

Everyone cheered, including me. "I've been telling them all about your special double chocolate chip cookies, Grandma," I said.

"Yeah," Spencer said licking his lips. "I can't wait to taste one!"

"Uh, gross!" Angela said, making a face. "Try not to drool on yourself."

Everyone laughed at that, including Spencer. "Have fun, kids," my mom said. "Don't burn the house down, okay?"

"I can't make any promises, Mrs. Hodges," Rusty joked.

Mom smiled and rolled her eyes. Then she left with Giggles. She'd promised to take him on a long walk when she went to run some errands around the neighborhood. That way he wouldn't try to eat everything as fast as we could bake it!

Grandma Hodges rubbed her hands together. "Okay, let's start with those double chocolate chip cookies, all right?"

"I'll get out the baking pans and mixing bowls," Obaasan said.

As she headed for the big cabinet in the pantry, I started helping Grandma Hodges take out ingredients. We'd gone shopping the previous afternoon for flour, eggs, milk, and everything else we'd need.

"Yum, brown sugar," Spencer said when he saw me set a package on the counter. "I love brown sugar."

"Hey!" Lola smacked his hand as he reached for the package. "Keep your dirty paws away from the food."

"Yeah, or at least wash your hands first," Pia said, wrinkling her nose. "They're filthy!"

Spencer spread out his hands. "No way. It'll give the baked goods more flavor." He snorted with laughter at his own joke. Cole and Rusty laughed, too.

"What's your name, young man?" Grandma Hodges asked Spencer.

"Peabody," Spencer replied.

That made everyone laugh. "His name's Spencer, Grandma," I said.

"Hmm." Grandma Hodges rubbed her chin. "Actually, Peabody seems to suit him better. I think I'll call him that, since he seems to prefer it. Now Peabody, let's get those hands of yours clean. You've got enough dirt on them to grow your own garden. In fact, why doesn't everyone get washed up?"

"My name's not really Peabody," Spencer said as she grabbed him by the elbow and dragged him over to the sink.

"What was that, Peabody?" Grandma Hodges asked. "I couldn't hear you over the water."

Spencer looked a little upset that his joke had backfired. Pia grinned and leaned toward me. "Your grandma's cool," she whispered. "She's totally putting Spencer—I mean Peabody—in his place! And I love how she color-coordinated her apron with her outfit!"

"Isn't she awesome?" I whispered back proudly.

Just then Obaasan returned with a stack of cookie trays and baking pans. "Here we go," she said. "These should work for those cookies. And if you'd like, I could show you how to make my sweet rice crackers after that."

"Really?" Lola smiled. "That would be great!"

A couple of the others looked interested, too. But I shook my head.

"Maybe some other time, Obaasan," I said. "Your rice crackers aren't on the list of stuff we're supposed to make today. I don't want to use up any of the ingredients we might need for the other

recipes." I shrugged. "Besides, most people at the bake sale probably won't even know what they are. We need to stick to our sure-fire best sellers, like Grandma's double chocolate chip cookies."

"Oh. All right." Obaasan brushed off her hands. "Well then, it is certainly crowded in here. I think I'll go outside and do some weeding. Call me if you need anything."

"Sure," I said. I was kind of surprised she didn't want to stay and help. Obaasan loves cooking. Then again, she loves working in the garden, too. "And don't worry, we should be okay. Grandma Hodges is here, remember?"

By then Grandma Hodges had finally finished getting Spencer to wash his hands. "All right," she said. "Now that Peabody's ready, it's time to bake!"

Spencer spoke up. "Would you stop calling me Peabody? My name is something else!"

"Oh, is *that* your name? All right 'Something Else,' it's time to bake," Grandma Hodges said with a chuckle. We all laughed. Everyone but Spencer, that is.

By dinnertime, we were all covered in flour and exhausted. But we also had a huge batch of all kinds of yummy stuff packed into boxes and ready for the bake sale. The baking session had been fun, even though Spencer kept driving everyone crazy by trying to lick the batter out of the bowls. He'd also managed to get his hands all yucky again within minutes, so we had to watch carefully to make sure he didn't touch anything. Luckily Grandma Hodges discovered

that Spencer actually had a talent for decorating cakes and cookies with a tube of frosting. He did such a good job that she finally even agreed to stop calling him Something Else.

"Wow," I said after everyone had left. "I can't believe that we baked enough stuff for both days of the bake sale."

Grandma Hodges smiled. "You kids worked hard," she said. "It always feels good to work for a good cause."

I smiled, thinking about how happy Irving would be once his garden was cleaned up and beautiful again. "Yeah," I said. "With everything we made today, plus that fancy pineapple upside-down cake, and the other team's car wash, we'll be sure to raise enough money to fix up *ten* gardens!"

Chapter 8

"Wow," Pia yawned. "I can't believe I'm up this early on a Saturday!"

Pia, Lola, and I were in my dad's car. He chuckled. "Should I drive you back home so you can get more beauty sleep?" he joked.

Pia sat up straight. "No!" she said. "I'm awake."

I giggled. Lola and I were sitting in the back seat on either side of Pia. All three of us had boxes of baked goods on our laps. The car's trunk was stuffed with more baked goods, a couple of folding chairs from Pia's apartment, and more stuff for the bake sale. I was feeling kind of anxious. We'd all worked so hard. I just wanted everything to go well.

"I hope Angela didn't forget to get here early with her dad's tables," I said, looking out the window as Dad turned onto the street where Emerson was.

"There she is!" Lola pointed. "Looks like Mrs. Clark is already helping her set up."

Pia leaned over for a better look. "Some of the car wash people are setting up, too," she said. "Look, there's Jesse—I can't believe she's up this early!"

Emerson Charter School was a large brick building set back from the street. There was a curved driveway where people could stop to drop off their kids right at the bottom of the front steps. The teachers' parking lot was on one side of the building, and the public parking lot was on the other. Mrs. Clark had already told us we could set up our bake sale in the public lot. The car wash would take place in the teachers' lot.

Soon Lola, Pia, and I were helping Angela and Mrs. Clark finish setting up the tables. A couple of other people arrived soon after that. They helped my dad finish unloading everything from our car.

"How's it going over there?" Pia called over to Jesse. Her team was just about done setting up on the other end of the driveway.

Jesse shot her a thumbs-up. "Awesome!" she called back. "We're going to raise a ton of money."

"Don't be so sure," Lola called with a grin. "Nobody in town will have any money left after they finish buying all of our amazing baked goods!"

"Yeah, right!" Jackie yelled back. "You wish!"

"Like anybody wants to pay for a bunch of lousy homemade cookies," Rory added.

"Think again," Angela yelled. "Jennifer's bringing a pineapple upside-down cake that's a guaranteed best seller!"

Just then I saw Jennifer's mom pulling into the driveway. Jennifer, Liza, and Gracie climbed out. Jennifer was carrying a white box. All three of them had glum faces.

"What's wrong?" I asked as they came over.

"Did you bring the cake?" Lola added.

Jennifer sighed loudly. "Yeah. But things

didn't go too well in the kitchen."

"We didn't put in enough baking soda," Liza said with a grimace. "The cake ended up sort of, you know, not rising—it's flat."

Jennifer opened the box. I saw they were right. The cake looked like a tire with half the air let out!

Jackie had run over to have a look. "Whoa," he said with a laugh. "Is that your best-selling cake? One thing's for sure. It does look upside down. Ooh, now I'm s-s-s-scared!" He raced back over to his own group, still laughing.

"Forget him," Angela said. "Who cares if one cake didn't turn out right? We still have lots of yummy treats."

She was right. But I still felt kind of annoyed. If Jennifer and her friends hadn't been trying to outdo everyone else as usual, this probably wouldn't have happened! Why couldn't they just have made brownies, like I'd asked for in the first place?

But I tried not to think about that. It was better to be flexible and have a sense of humor about problems, like Grandma Hodges said.

"Even if it doesn't look right, it probably still tastes good," I said. "Just put it over there with the other stuff."

Only one person bought a slice of the pineapple upside-down cake—Liza's older brother. And he only ate one bite before throwing the rest away.

But that didn't matter. People loved the rest of our food. We had tons of customers all day long.

The car wash was going well, too. It looked
like none of Jesse's group got to rest, either.
They were all kept busy soaping, scrubbing, and
rinsing the cars that lined up in the parking lot
waiting for their turn.

Jesse came over to us at the end of the day.
Lola, Rusty, and I were counting the cash in our
box. "Whew! I thought I'd never get a break,"
she said. "I'm so tired. But it's worth it. We made
so much money, and it's only our very first day!"

"How much did you make?" Lola challenged Jesse, crossing her arms over her chest.

When Jesse told her the number, my mouth dropped open. "Wow, that's, like, forty dollars more than we've made so far!" I exclaimed.

"Oh, really?" Jesse had a smug look on her face. "Well, I can't say I'm surprised. I told you the car wash was a better idea than the bake sale!" She looked back at her team. "Oh look, there's *another* customer. I'd better go—ta ta!"

Chapter 9

Jesse skipped back over to her side. I felt defeated as I watched her go.

"Don't mind her, Amy," Lola said with a frown. "This bake sale was a great idea."

"Anyway, we'll beat her in the end," Rusty added. "There are only so many dirty cars in this city. But there's no limit to how much people can eat!"

Lola laughed. "Right," she said. "But just to make sure, we need to step things up for tomorrow."

"Yeah," Rusty agreed. "We need, like, a gimmick or something."

"I've got it!" Lola's eyes lit up. "How about a jingle? We can stand out front and sing it to anyone passing by. That'll bring more people in for sure!"

"A jingle?" I said doubtfully. I didn't see how that would make any difference.

But Rusty was nodding. "Great idea!" he said. "Can you write one?"

"Definitely," Lola said confidently. "I'll come up with something tonight and have it ready by tomorrow. Just don't be late tomorrow. You'll need to learn it before the sale starts."

❀ ❀ ❀

"I'm not sure a jingle will do any good," I said with a sigh. After dinner that night, I was sitting at the kitchen table with both my grandmothers. The rest of the family had already left the room.

Obaasan reached over and patted my hand. "You're right, Little Mitsukai," she said. "You shouldn't need gimmicks if your product is good enough to stand on its own."

"Oh, I don't know about that," Grandma Hodges said with a wink. "Every little bit helps! A jingle could be fun. After all, if you don't attract people's attention to begin with, then they might never get the chance to see just how great your product really is."

"I never thought about it that way," I admitted. "Maybe a jingle *is* a good idea. Thanks, Grandma Hodges!"

First thing the next morning, Lola taught us the jingle she'd written. Well, most of us anyway. Jennifer and her friends hadn't gotten there yet.

"Figures *they'd* be late," Cole muttered. "They might not even show up today since their cake was such a bust yesterday."

"Never mind them," Lola said. "I'll teach them the jingle whenever they get here. Here's how it goes . . ."

First she hummed the tune. Then she helped us memorize the words. They were pretty simple:

Please would you buy some cake or cookies?
Won't you please try some cake or cookies?
Won't you please buy them?
Won't you please try them?
They're so sat-is-fy-ing!

"That's pretty catchy," Pia said after we'd all sung it a couple of times. "I bet it will get lots of people to stop and take a look."

"Just sing it as loudly as you can," Lola advised.

So we did. And Pia was right. Everyone seemed to love our new jingle! People flocked to buy even more of our baked goods than they had the day before.

Mrs. Clark wandered over just as a customer was hurrying off with a whole batch of sugar cookies.

"Congratulations, kids," she said with a smile. "Looks like people are completely charmed by your jingle! That was a wonderful idea."

She was looking at me as she said it. I didn't want to take credit for Lola's idea, so I pointed to her. "Lola wrote it," I said. "It was all her idea. Well, and Rusty's, too."

Just then another car pulled into the driveway. "Look, I think Jennifer's finally here!" Angela said.

"Glad she could make it," Cole said sarcastically.

Jennifer and her friends climbed out of the car. Each of them was holding a big white box.

"Sorry we're late," Gracie called out as the three of them hurried over. "We were busy baking over at Jennifer's house all morning."

"Yeah. We made brownies, see?" Jennifer flipped open her box. Inside were stacks of chocolate and butterscotch brownies.

Liza nodded. "We got up extra early this

morning to make sure they were ready, but they still took a little longer than we thought."

I was amazed. I never would have expected the three of them to do something like that. "Wow, thanks, you guys," I said. "This is great!"

Spencer grabbed a brownie out of Jennifer's box before anyone could stop him. "Mmm!" he said as he took a big bite. "Whoa, these are awesome!"

Jennifer smirked proudly. "Yeah, they are, aren't they?" she said. "We might want to charge a little extra for them since they're so good. We used this special organic vanilla from Madagascar."

She kept going on and on about how perfect her brownies were. But as we set out the brownies, people started buying them right away. For once, I didn't mind her bragging one bit!

Chapter 10

Believe it or not, Jennifer and her friends are actually pretty good singers. Soon our jingle was attracting even more attention than before. It was hard to keep up with all the people who wanted to buy our treats.

Mrs. Clark walked over as I was selling a slice of pie and several brownies to a man with two young daughters.

"How are things going?" Mrs. Clark asked.

"We're running out of napkins," I told her breathlessly.

She nodded. "I'll see what I can find in the cafeteria. Be right back."

Mrs. Clark hurried into the school building. Just then I saw Jesse coming toward us from her side of the parking lot.

"What's all the singing over here?" she demanded. "I thought this was supposed to be a bake sale, not a rock concert!"

She sounded a little cranky. When I looked over toward the car wash, I figured out why. There weren't very many customers over there.

Liza was standing right next to me. "Sorry, we don't have time to chat now, Jesse," she said. "We're too busy." Then she went back to singing our jingle as she packed up some muffins for a customer.

Jesse scowled. Then she stomped off back to her side without another word.

I watched as she huddled with some of her team. They all peeked over at us, looking upset.

A few minutes later there was a lull in our stream of customers. I wandered over to Cole and Lola.

"I feel kinda bad that Jesse's group didn't have that many customers this morning," I admitted to my friends.

Cole shrugged. "Forget it," he said. "It's not our fault people would rather hang out at our bake sale than their car wash."

Lola grinned. "Yeah. Or that our jingle is so great that people can't resist it!"

"I know," I said. "Still, we're all supposed to be working together for the same cause, right?"

Before the others could answer, we heard a new sound coming from the other parking lot. Singing!

I gasped. "They're singing our jingle!" I exclaimed.

"Not quite," Cole said grimly. "It sounds like

they changed the words . . ."

He was right. The tune was the same, but the lyrics were different. I listened carefully to what they were singing:

Please would you let us wash your car?
Please let us make you look like a star.
Won't you please try us?
Don't just drive by us.
You'll be sat-is-fied!

"They stole our jingle!" Lola cried, outraged. "I won't let them get away with this!"

"Lola, wait . . ." I began.

But it was too late. Lola was already stomping off toward the car washers.

"Come on," Pia cried. "Let's go with her."

Almost everyone rushed off after Lola. Only Spencer and Angela stayed at our tables with me. I wasn't sure what to do because there were still customers who needed to be helped.

"Stay here and keep an eye on everything,

okay?" I begged them. Then I ran after the others.

When I got there, they were confronting the car washers. "You can't use our jingle!" Lola yelled at Jesse.

Jesse crossed her arms over her chest. "Says who?"

"Guys . . ." I began.

"You're just a bunch of sore losers," Jennifer said with a sniff. "Stealing our song was totally lame."

"Please, everyone!" Maya cried. "Don't argue, okay?"

She seemed to be the only one besides me who didn't want to argue. Everyone else started yelling at one another. Our group complained

about the others using our jingle. The car washers yelled about us stealing their customers. Voices got louder and angrier.

Then a car pulled into the school driveway. It stopped right in the middle, halfway between the bake sale and the car wash.

"Look, a customer!" Rusty cried, pointing.

"Stay back," Jesse yelled. "This one's ours!"

"No way!" Jennifer retorted.

Everyone ran over to the car just as a woman got out with her young daughter.

"Please would you let us wash your car!" Jesse sang loudly at her. The rest of her group joined in, singing their version of the jingle.

In response, Lola and some of the others started singing our bake sale jingle at the woman and her daughter. Actually, it was more like shouting than singing.

The woman looked startled. Her daughter started to cry.

"Oh, my!" the woman exclaimed.

At least I think that's what she said. I could

only tell by reading her lips. The singing was too loud for me to hear her.

The woman grabbed her daughter and hustled her back into the car. Seconds later she was driving away at top speed.

"Now look what you did!" Jackie yelled. "You scared them away!"

"Nuh-uh," Gracie shouted back. "It was you guys who scared them!"

I put my hands over my ears. This was crazy! Everyone was out of control. We were all blaming and accusing one another.

This wasn't what community activism was supposed to be about. What was I going to do now?

Chapter 11

A loud whistle broke up the arguing. Mrs. Clark had finally returned from inside.

"What's going on out here?" she cried, setting down the armful of napkins she was carrying. Mrs. Musgrove was right behind her.

Everyone started talking at once. But Mrs. Musgrove held up her hand.

"One at a time," she said sternly.

Lola and Jesse and a few other people took turns explaining. Soon both teachers were shaking their heads.

"You're losing sight of what this project is supposed to be about," Mrs. Clark said sadly.

"We're raising money for a community garden—a place that's supposed to bring people together. Remember?" asked Mrs. Musgrove.

Jesse bit her lip and shot a look at Lola. Lola

glanced back. A few others shuffled their feet or mumbled.

Jesse was the first one to apologize, which was a really big deal because everyone knows she hates to admit when she's wrong. "I'm sorry," she said. "Um, I guess this is mostly my fault." She took a deep breath and stepped toward Lola. "I shouldn't have stolen your jingle. I'm really sorry."

"It's okay," Lola said with a shrug. "Your lyrics were actually pretty good."

"Look," I spoke up. "It's like Mrs. Clark and

Mrs. Musgrove said. We shouldn't be fighting over customers. We should share them instead."

"Huh?" Spencer said.

"Maybe Jesse can send her customers over for a sweet treat while they're waiting for their cars to be washed," I explained. "And we can suggest a shiny car wash to our bake sale customers."

"That's a great idea, Amy," Maya said with a smile.

"Yeah," Rusty agreed. Most of the others nodded, too.

"Good." Mrs. Clark smiled. "Then let's get back to work. We've got funds to raise—together!"

❀ ❀ ❀

The rest of the afternoon was a big success. By the end of the day, both of our cash boxes were full.

"I'll count up the cash from the bake sale group while Mrs. Musgrove tallies the car wash group's total. We'll let you know how much each team raised in just a minute," Mrs. Clark said.

"Cool," Lola said. "But don't divide it by team,

okay? Just tell us the total amount both fund-raisers raised together. After all, this isn't a competition." She glanced around at the rest of us. "Right, guys?"

I cheered. So did almost everyone else.

Mrs. Clark smiled. "It's a deal," she agreed.

On Sunday night, I spent most of dinner telling my family all about the fund-raiser. They'd all stopped by that afternoon to buy some treats and get the car washed. But there was still a lot more to fill them in on.

"Sounds like the weekend was a great success after all," Harabujy said with a smile.

My dad nodded. "You'll be able to do a terrific job sprucing up Irving's garden next weekend."

"Definitely," I agreed. Then I turned toward Grandma Hodges. "Thanks so much for helping us plan it all, Grandma Hodges! We couldn't have done it without you."

"It was my pleasure," Grandma Hodges

replied. "I only wish I didn't have to go home tomorrow. I'd love to help with the gardening!"

"I wish you could stay, too." I felt a pang of sadness. In all the excitement, I'd almost forgotten she was going back to Wilkerson the next day. "I'm sure you're as awesome at gardening as you are at everything else!"

My dad chuckled. "Oh, I don't know about that," he joked. "I seem to remember that my father was the one who always watered the houseplants."

"That's because I was too busy trying to keep your little mischievous behind out of trouble," Grandma Hodges exclaimed. But her eyes were twinkling. Mom and Harabujy and I laughed. I glanced over at Obaasan, but she was looking down at her plate. I guessed she hadn't heard what Dad and Grandma Hodges had just said. In fact, now that I thought about it, she'd been awfully quiet all during dinner.

"Anyway, Mrs. Clark is going to call Irving and let him know how much money we raised," I said. "I bet he'll be really happy."

Grandma Hodges reached across the table and squeezed my hand. "He will be, baby," she said with a smile. "And it's all thanks to you and your friends—and some good old-fashioned community activism."

After dinner, Dad and I volunteered to wash up. "I'm going to miss Grandma Hodges," I told him as I carried some dishes over to the sink.

"Me too," he said. "But she'll come visit again soon. Or maybe during your next school break we can go to Wilkerson to see her and Grandpa."

"That would be great!" Then I remembered something I'd wanted to ask him. "Hey Dad," I said. "Have you noticed that Obaasan's acting kind of weird and uh, you know, extra quiet today? Actually, maybe not just today. She didn't want to help us bake the other day, either, which seemed strange . . ."

Dad set down the serving dish he was rinsing and turned to face me. "Yes, I have noticed that Obaasan hasn't quite been herself these last few days."

"Really?" I felt a flash of worry. "What do you think is wrong?"

Chapter 12

"Well, I haven't spoken with her about it," Dad said. "But I suspect she's feeling a bit neglected because you've been spending all of your free time with Grandma Hodges."

"What?" I cried out in surprise. "What do you mean?"

"Obaasan is used to being one of the most important people in your life," Dad said gently. "And, well, she might not be feeling that way right now."

I felt terrible. I definitely hadn't meant to ignore Obaasan! It was just that Grandma Hodges was only visiting for a short time. Still, now that Dad had pointed it out, I saw how Obaasan could have felt left out.

"Um, can you finish washing up without me?" I asked, setting down the forks I was holding. "I think I need to go talk with Obaasan."

"Sure, go ahead."

I rushed out of the kitchen. My mom and Grandma Hodges were in the living room.

"There you are, Amy," Grandma Hodges said. "I was just going to head upstairs to start packing my things. Want to help?"

"Maybe in a little while," I said. "Have you guys seen Obaasan?"

"I think she said she was going out to the garden," Mom said.

"Thanks." As soon as I went outside, I spotted Obaasan. She was picking flowers from her neatly tended beds out front.

"Little Mitsukai!" she said in surprise when I raced over. "What is it?"

Now that I was there, I suddenly felt a little bit tongue-tied. "Um, what are you doing out here?" I asked.

She held up the flowers she was holding. "I'm picking a bouquet for your Grandma Hodges. I thought she could take the flowers home to

Grandpa Hodges, since
he didn't get to come
see us."

"That's a great idea,"
I said. "Maybe I can
help you?"

"Of course."

I plucked a pretty
white flower and
handed it to her. Then
I took a deep breath.
I could hear my heart
thumping nervously.

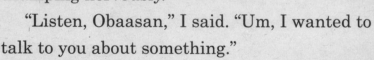

"Listen, Obaasan," I said. "Um, I wanted to
talk to you about something."

"What is it?" she asked.

"It's about Grandma Hodges," I said. "Well,
actually it's about you. And me. I'm really sorry
I haven't been spending much time with you
this past week." Now that I'd started, my words
came out all in a rush. "It's just that Grandma
Hodges lives so far away, and I only see her once

in a while . . . I guess maybe I sort of forgot about you for a while just because you're always here. But I should never do that. I love having you live with us. I love all the fun stuff we do together. And I especially love *you*. So I'm really sorry for ignoring you while Grandma Hodges was here."

Obaasan looked surprised. "Oh! I love you, too, Little Mitsukai," she said, reaching out for a hug. "But there's no need to apologize. I understand, and of course it's important for you to spend time with your other grandmother. I'm glad you got to know her better on this visit— and I'm glad I did, too. Your Grandma Hodges is a very special lady."

"I know. I'm lucky to have *two* super special grandmas," I said, hugging her back.

I was glad I'd apologized. Even though she'd said I didn't *have* to apologize, I could tell Obaasan was glad I had.

The following Saturday morning, the entire fourth grade gathered at Irving's garden. We'd used our fund-raising money to buy tons of gardening supplies. There were shovels, wheelbarrows, new plants and seeds, and much more. Everyone was working hard and having fun.

Irving was there, too. He just kept thanking us over and over again, seeming delighted and a little overwhelmed with what was happening. Some other people from the neighborhood had stopped by to help once they saw what we were doing. That made Irving even happier!

"This is so much fun," Jesse said. She tipped a watering can over some freshly planted flowers. "And the garden is looking a lot better already! I'm glad you thought of this project, Amy."

I smiled. "Me too," I said. "And I'm glad we're all working together."

Rusty hurried over holding a big potted plant. "Mrs. Clark said we should plant this over here," he said. "Can you do it, Amy? I already promised to help put up the new tomato cages."

"Sure." I took the plant from him. "How far apart should this be from those flowers?"

Rusty shrugged. "Beats me." He hurried away.

"Never mind. I know who to ask," I said to Jesse. I looked around the busy garden. Lola, Maya, and Pia were pulling some weedy vines off the chain-link fence. Jennifer and her friends were painting a fence. Evelyn and Stanley were trimming some overgrown bushes. A bunch of others were weeding or raking or planting things.

Finally I spotted exactly who I was looking for.

Obaasan was over by a tree helping Cole and a couple of the other kids prune dead or broken branches. I'd invited her along to our gardening day. After all, she is the best gardener I know!

I hurried over and asked for her help with the plant Rusty had given me. "Let's see what we can do, Little Mitsukai," she said, brushing the dirt off her hands.

Soon we were working in the dirt together.

"That looks great," I told her as she patted down the dirt around the base of the plant. "Thanks, Obaasan."

"It's my pleasure," she replied with a smile.

Just then a frisky dog raced over to see what we were doing. Irving was right behind her.

"Hi there, Babe," I said, patting the friendly dog. "I wish I could've brought Giggles along to play with you." I laughed. "But I didn't want you two to run off again!"

Irving chuckled. "Must admit I'm glad they did run off together that first time," he said. "Otherwise I never would have met you. Can't thank you enough for helping to make all this happen!"

I smiled, knowing he was right. Even though losing Giggles had seemed like the most terrible day of my life, it had led to something good—this amazing class project. I reached into my pocket and pulled out a digital camera from the front pocket of my overalls.

"Say cheese!" I said to Irving and Obaasan, snapping a picture of them.

Even though I was busy, I was trying to remember to take plenty of pictures. I wanted to have lots of "before and after" photos of the garden for my scrapbook. I also wanted to send some to Grandma Hodges so she could see how our community project turned out and how all of our fund-raising efforts paid off.

Then I put the camera away and went back to work. There was still a lot to get done. After all, it wasn't easy being green.

But it sure was fun!

The 4th Grade Fund-raiser

BRIGHT IDEA!

The Car Wash Team

WHO WILL RAISE THE MOST MONEY?

SAVE THE GARDEN!
BAKE SALE

The Bake Sale Team

Sweet Success!

We Saved the Garden!

Irving, me, and Obaasan!

I DIG GARDENING!

Stop and Smell the Roses...

Everyone worked together to save the garden.

♡ About the Authors ❀

Kim Wayans and Kevin Knotts are actors and writers (and wife and husband) who live in Los Angeles, California. Kevin was raised on a ranch in Oklahoma, and Kim grew up in the heart of New York City. They were inspired to write the Amy Hodgepodge series by their beautiful nieces and nephews—many of whom are mixed-race children—and by the fact that when you look around the world today, it's more of a hodgepodge than ever.